Seattle ABC

A Larry Gets Lost book

Written by John Skewes and Robert Schwartz
Illustrated by John Skewes

SASQUATCH BOOKS
SEATTLE

Text and illustrations copyright
© 2009 by John Skewes

Printed in China
Published by Sasquatch Books
Distributed by PGW/Perseus
15 14 13 12 11 10 09   9 8 7 6 5 4 3 2 1

Book design by Mint Design

Library of Congress Cataloging-in-Publication Data

Skewes, John.
  Seattle ABC : a Larry gets lost book / illustrated by John Skewes ;
written by John Skewes and Robert Schwartz.
     p. cm.
  ISBN-13: 978-1-57061-590-0
  ISBN-10: 1-57061-590-X
 1. Seattle (Wash.)--Juvenile literature. 2. Alphabet books. I.
Schwartz, Robert. II. Title.
  F899.S44S59 2009
  979.7'772--dc22
                          2008044903

SASQUATCH BOOKS
119 South Main Street, Suite 400
Seattle, WA 98104
(206) 467-4300

www.sasquatchbooks.com
custserv@sasquatchbooks.com

This is **Larry.**

This is **Pete.**

They like looking for **letters**
as they walk down the street.

A is for **aquarium,** for fish of all sizes.

**Evergreen Point
Floating Bridge**

B

is for **bridges** that
float or stand up!

Fremont Bridge

is for **coffee,** found
on every corner.

D is for **docks,**
where people
park boats.

E is for **evergreens,** which stay green all winter.

F

is for **ferry boats,** which carry cars across the water.

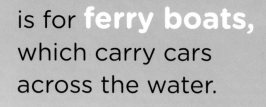

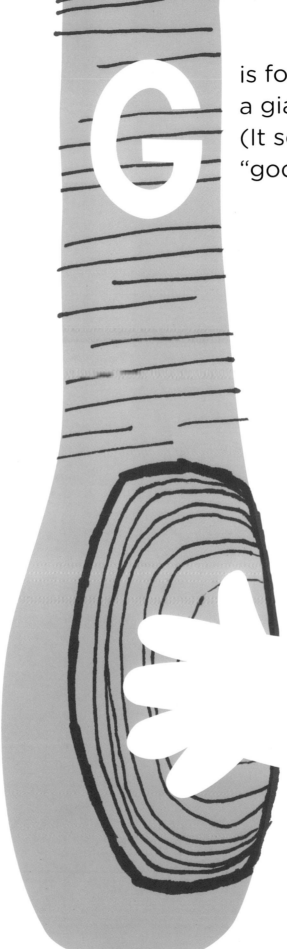

G is for **geoduck**, a giant clam. (It sounds like "gooey-duck.")

H

is for **houseboats** and **hydroplanes.**
Both of them float, but hydroplanes move
fast. Houseboats stay put.

Lake Union

Seafair Hydroplane Races,
Lake Washington

I

is for **Interstate 5,**
Seattle's biggest road.

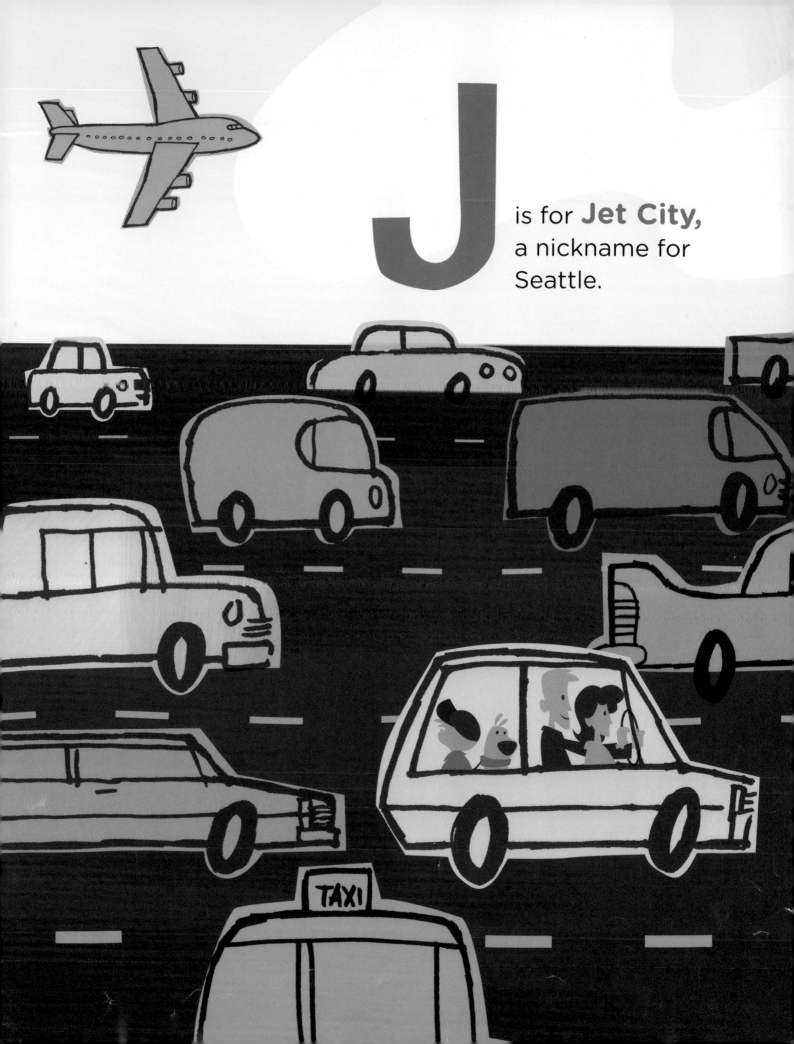

J

is for **Jet City**, a nickname for Seattle.

K is for **King County.**

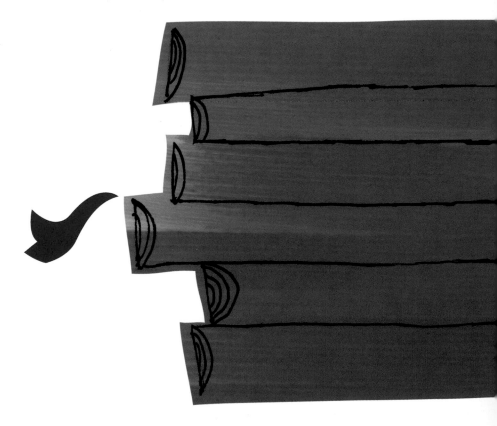

L is for logs.

M is for **monorail.**

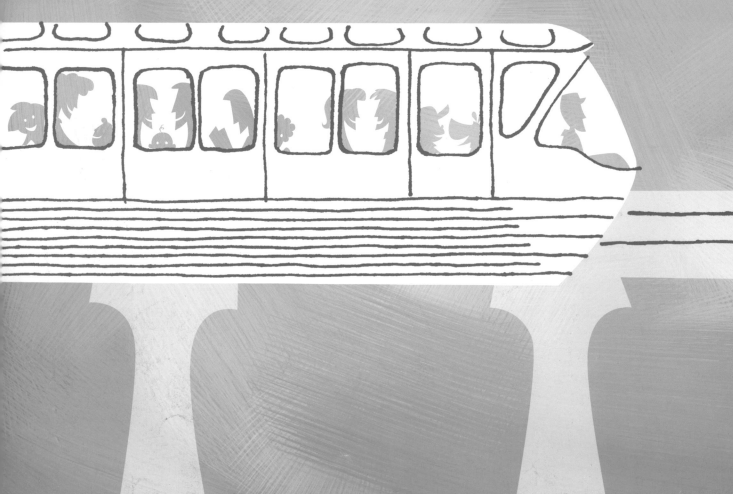

Next stop: **Space** **N**eedle.

is for **orcas,**
who sometimes
swim into
Elliott Bay.

P is for **Pike Place Market,** where you'll find fresh things to eat.

Q

is for **Queen Anne Hill.**

R is for **rain.**

Time for an
umbrella?
No, not yet.

S

is for the **sculptures** that fill the Sculpture Park.

Olympic Sculpture Park

T

is for **totem pole,** a sculpture made from a tree.

U

is for **umbrella.**
(Now it's time.)

Alaskan Way Viaduct

V
is for **viaduct,** a road
above the ground.

CANADA

W

is for

W is for

WaSh
X
ington

IDAHO

X marks the spot where Seattle,
Pete, and Larry can be found.

OREGON

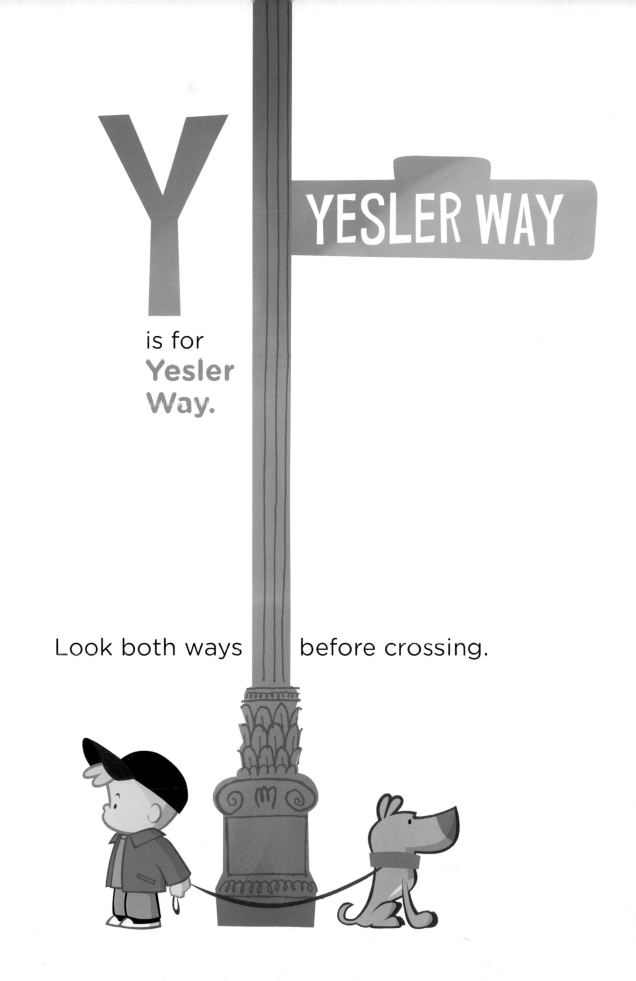

Y

is for **Yesler Way.**

Look both ways before crossing.

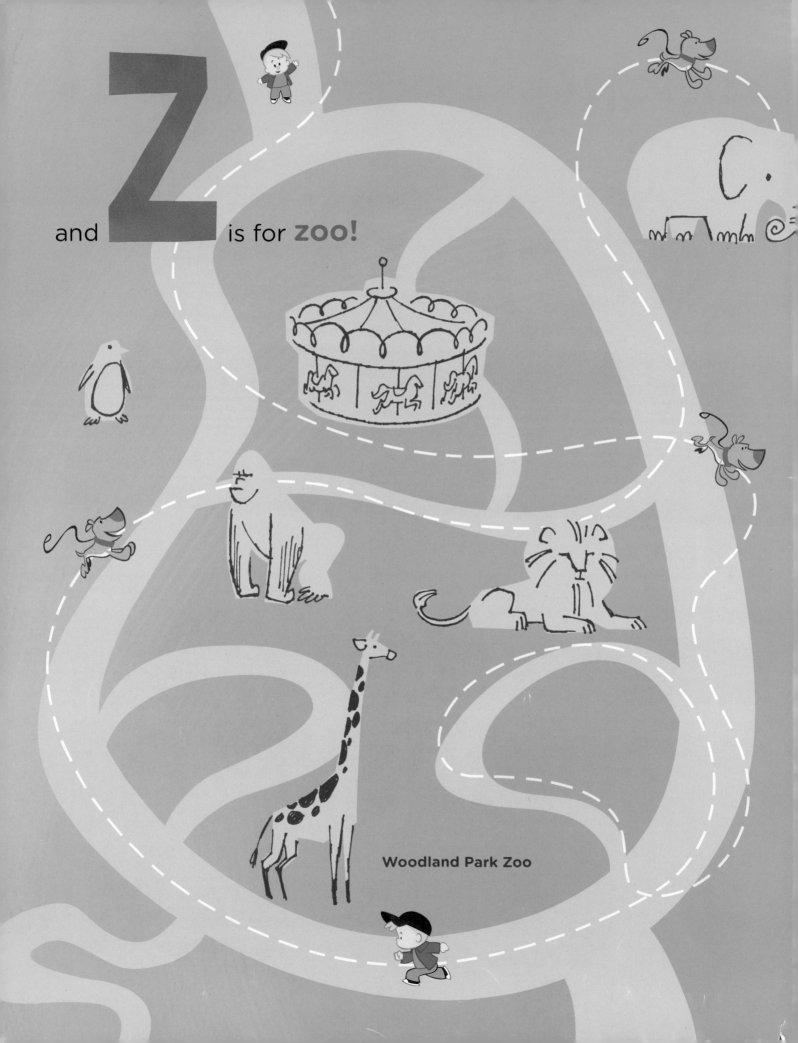

and **Z** is for **zoo!**

Woodland Park Zoo

How many **letters** do you see around you?